Walt Disney's
AMERICAN CLASSICS
The Legend of Sleepy Hollow

Twin Books

MALLARD
PRESS

In the Catskill Mountains, many, many years ago, there was a peaceful little green valley called Sleepy Hollow. One day a tall, skinny stranger came to the village there. He was an odd-looking fellow, and resembled a scarecrow from a cornfield.

"Whoever is that?" one man asked.

"Shhh," whispered his neighbor. "He's the new schoolmaster!"

2

This peculiar-looking schoolmaster had an even more peculiar name—Ichabod Crane!

But he was popular with his pupils, and he was especially kind to those whose mothers were good cooks.

Often, he visited his students in the evening, and oh, how the stacks of food disappeared then! It was a delight to cook for a man who ate so well, and who said "Thank you " with such style.

He was admired by everyone…

... well, almost everyone. The one person who did *not* admire the schoolmaster was Brom Bones. From the very start, Brom didn't care for Ichabod Crane.

Brom was big and strong. He could out-ride, out-wrestle and *out-trick* anyone.

6

Now Brom suspected that the schoolmaster was very superstitious, so he went into the school late one night and turned things topsy-turvy. Sure enough, when Ichabod entered the room the next morning, he cried out, "All the goblins in the county must have held a meeting here!"

One day Ichabod met Katrina Van Tassel, the beautiful daughter of the richest farmer in the valley. One look at her stole his heart away.

But there was another whose heart pined for Katrina—Brom Bones.

Ichabod spent endless hours dreaming of Katrina. Indeed, his thoughts bounced back and forth between Katrina's beautiful face and her father's piles of money.

"Why," sighed Ichabod, "if I could win the hand of Katrina, I would have the most beautiful wife in all of Sleepy Hollow *and* I'd be the master of the Van Tassel Farm!"

Katrina flirted with both Brom Bones and Ichabod Crane. Brom grew more jealous of his new rival every day, but each time he was about to get his hands on Ichabod, Katrina appeared.

"I'll get him one of these days," Brom thought to himself.

When Halloween night arrived, Farmer Van Tassel gave a huge party, as he'd done every year. Katrina had sent Ichabod a very special invitation.

When Ichabod arrived, Brom Bones was already there, but Ichabod gave his rival scarcely a glance. Instead, he went straight to Katrina's side, and presented himself with his courtliest bow.

"Good evening, my dear," said Ichabod. Katrina just blushed.

The orchestra struck up a happy tune, and in a moment Ichabod and Katrina were gliding across the floor. All evening they swung and bounded and swooped about the room.

Brom Bones just sat in the corner and glared at the merry couple, for even though he wanted to cut in and claim Katrina as his own, he knew he couldn't dance as well as Ichabod.

Ichabod was definitely the man of the hour, and Brom had to agree that it was so. "There must be a way," he thought, "to put this schoolish scarecrow of a man in his place! But how?"

During a break in the music, Ichabod knocked over a salt shaker, and had to throw a pinch over his shoulder, "to ward off goblins," he said. Carefree as he looked, he could never be completely relaxed in any situation, for he was terribly superstitious.

Brom suddenly grinned devilishly.

"It's Halloween night!" said Farmer Van Tasssel. "Someone tell us a ghost story!" Brom Bones jumped at the chance, certain now that Ichabod was mortally afraid of spooks of all kinds.

"At midnight," Brom roared, "the ghosts gather for their nightly jamboree! The worst one of all is the Headless Horseman, who haunts the old graveyard!"

The clock struck twelve, and a chill went down Ichabod's spine.

"On Halloween night," thundered Brom, "the Horseman hunts for a head to steal from its owner! But he can never cross the old Hollow bridge. Your only chance is to get there before he does. Beware! His sword has chopped off many a head!" And to show what the Horseman would do, Brom grabbed the head off a scarecrow and thrust it in Ichabod's face.

Ichabod was panic-stricken.

Quaking with fright, Ichabod thought of the spooky ride home alone. He hated to start down the deep, dark Hollow.

Finally, when all the other guests had gone, he knew that he also must go. He gave his thanks to the Van Tassels, and mounted his old horse.

"G-g-good night," he called in a quavery voice. Off he rode into the deep Hollow. The woods grew darker and darker.

The night sounds seemed to be getting louder and louder, and closer and closer. Ichabod tried to whistle, but his throat was dry. The wind blowing through the broken reeds made eerie sounds, like something breathing down the back of his neck.

"Faster, old horse! Faster!" he urged, but it was no use.

Suddenly an owl hooted, and the poor old horse bolted frantically
down the Hollow, with a terrified Ichabod clinging to him for dear life!

Ichabod managed to stay on, but just as he approached the graveyard, a towering figure on a fearsome black horse loomed before him in the darkness.

The monstrous horse rose up on its hind legs with a sound like thunder. It was the Headless Horseman!

Ichabod kicked and flailed at his poor old horse, and it ran into the darkness, out of control. Again and again, the Headless Horseman slashed at Ichabod, swinging his huge, sharp sword!

Whoosh! *Whoosh*! *Whoosh*!
Ichabod ducked down in his saddle, as the
sword sliced through the air just over his head.

"If only I can reach the bridge," thought Ichabod, for at the bridge the Horseman's power would end.

"Faster! Faster!" Ichabod shrieked, as the old horse scrambled frantically toward the bridge.

As he neared the end of the bridge, Ichabod glanced back to see if the fiend was still following. To his horror, he saw the Horseman rise up in his stirrups and hurl something through the air. Ichabod stared, completely unable to cry out, for coming directly at him was a grinning HEAD!

40

The morning after Halloween, the schoolmaster was missing. He had never missed breakfast before, but today he did not show up. Later that morning, someone found Ichabod's hat near the bridge. Not far away they also found a shattered pumpkin—and no one could say why *that* was there.

There was no sign of Ichabod Crane.
In fact, he was never seen again.

Shortly thereafter, Brom Bones took Katrina Van Tassel for his bride, and the Hollow settled down. As for Ichabod—well, some folks swear that he was spirited away by the Headless Horseman. Others say that he just moved to another county.

But every once in a while, a traveler drops by the inn to say that he has just heard the voice of Ichabod Crane, wailing in the Sleepy Hollow moonlight.

First published in the United States of America in 1989 by The Mallard Press.

Mallard Press and its accompanying design and logo are trademarks of BDD Promotional Book Company, Inc.

Produced by Twin Books
15 Sherwood Place
Greenwich, CT 06830
USA

ISBN 0-792-45052-3

Designed, edited and illustrated by American Graphic Systems, San Francisco

Printed in Hong Kong in 1989